躍變・龍城——九龍城主題步行徑｜社區繪本 09（九龍城篇）
Kowloon City in Transformation – Kowloon City Themed Walking Trail｜Picture Book No.9: Kowloon City

繪本名稱：媽媽的潮州雜貨店
Mum's Teochew Grocery Store

編輯：丘前朗、周嘉晴
Edited by Frandie Yau, Kylie Chow

插畫：塗鴉子
Illustrated by Hazel Lau

設計及排版：塗鴉子、林紫茵、羅美齡
Designed by Hazel Lau, Traci Lam, Amelia Loh

編審：陳詠琳、鄭詠恩
Reviewed by Gwyneth Chan, Vivian Cheng

督印人：何穎儀
Supervised by Joyce Ho

策劃及出版：躍變・龍城——九龍城主題步行徑
Published by Kowloon City in Transformation –
Kowloon City Themed Walking Trail

出版者：萬里機構出版有限公司
Published by Wan Li Book Company Limited

發行：香港聯合書刊物流有限公司
Issued by SUP Publishing Logistics Hong Kong Limited

承印：中華商務彩色印刷有限公司
Printed by C&C Offset Printing Co., Ltd

印量：1,000
1,000 copies in print

出版日期：2024年6月初版
First edition June 2024

九龍城主題步行徑辦公室 Office：
九龍馬頭涌真善美村低座一樓
1/F, Lower Block, Chun Seen Mei Chuen,
Ma Tau Chung, Kowloon

躍變・龍城體驗館
九龍譚公道115號運通大廈地下5號舖
Information Centre
Shop No.5, Ground Floor, Wan Tung Building,
No.115 Tam Kung Road, Kowloon

電話 Tel：+852 3183 0928
電郵 Email：kctwt@skhwc.org.hk
傳真 Fax：+852 3104 9911
網址 Website：kjowlooncitywalkingtrail.hk

 九龍城主題步行徑
 Kowloon City Walking Trail

國際書號 ISBN：978-962-14-7562-6
定價 Price：HK$78.00

步行徑舉辦了九龍城泰潮文化繪本插畫師招募計劃，並協助兩位獲選的插畫師完成繪本創作、出版及發行，以文字及插畫細訴九龍城的泰潮故事，連繫社區。
Kowloon City Themed Walking Trail organised a recruitment programme of illustrators for the Kowloon City Thai and Teochew Culture Picture Book. Two illustrators were selected and provided with assistance in creating, publishing and distributing the picture books. The programme aimed to engage with the community by narrating the Thai and Teochew stories of Kowloon City through words and illustrations.

媽媽的潮州雜貨店
Mum's Teochew Grocery Store

主辦 Organised by

躍變●龍城
Kowloon City in Transformation

營運 Operated by

香港聖公會福利協會
HONG KONG SHENG KUNG HUI WELFARE COUNCIL

贊助 Funded by

URF
市區更新基金
Urban Renewal Fund

媽媽要退休了!
她要把潮州雜貨店交給我……
Mum is getting retired! She wants to hand over
the Teochew grocery store to me...

怎麼辦？我沒有經營雜貨店的經驗！
I have never run a grocery store before!
What should I do?

gian²
囝*！
Sweetie!

*潮州人對子女的稱呼。
The name Teochew people use for their children.

魚飯 Cold Fish

又稱「凍魚」，常見於潮州打冷，當中不含米飯。

Also known as "Cold Fish", a common food in Teochow late-night meals. It does not contain rice.

薄殼 Baby Mussels

潮汕時令海產，通常在端午後至中秋當造，特別稀有。

A rare seasonal seafood in Chaoshan. It is usually in season between the Dragon Boat Festival and the Mid-Autumn Festival.

這些是潮州傳統的特色食物。
These are traditional Teochew specialities.

鹹菜 Salted Vegetables

用芥菜製成的醃製蔬菜，口感帶鹹、酥脆，引人食慾。
Pickled vegetables made from mustard leaves. It tastes salty, crispy and appetising.

潮州粥 Teochew Porridge

潮州人會用白米煮潮州粥（糜），充滿米香及米粒口感。
Teochew people cook Teochew porridge with white rice. The smell and grain texture of rice are rich.

這些是潮州粿和糕點。
These are Teochew pastries.

紅桃粿 Red Peach Cake

潮汕地區的傳統特色小食。節日時人們
用此來祈禱家庭安康、生活愉快。

A traditional snack in Chaoshan. People use
them to pray for good fortune and joy in
life during festivals and celebrations.

鼠殼粿 Rat Shell Cake

加入了鼠殼草製作而成的糕點。顏色
深綠，柔軟香甜。

A Teochew pastry which made from
Jersey Cudweed. It is dark green in
colour, soft and sweet.

在節慶場合能看見！
We can see them during festivals!

月糕 Mooncake

潮州傳統糕點之一。人們會在中秋節製作月糕。

One of the traditional pastries in Teochew culture. It is typically made during Mid-Autumn Festival.

韭菜粿 Chive Dumpling

其中一種最常見的潮州粿。常煎香食用，外皮香脆。

One of the most common Teochew rice cakes, often served as fried chive dumplings, which are crispy.

這些是不同種類的潮式醬料。

These are different kinds of Teochew condiments and sauces.

有豆醬、辣椒油、橄欖菜等。

Including soy bean sauce, chili oil,
pickled mustard leaves with olive, etc.

請給我兩斤米！
Two catties of rice, please!

這個米秤怎麼用？
How does the balance work?

盛惠三十元！
Thirty dollars, please!

謝謝！
Thank you!

短短一個月，媽媽已經將店裏的
知識傳授給我。原來經營雜貨店
沒有想像中那麼複雜。

Mum taught me how to run the store in just one
month. It was easier than I expected.

好吧！就交給我吧！

All right! Just leave it to me!

新潮飯店

合潮

Nga Tsin Long Road
衙前塱道 2 ◆ 32

這段日子裏，我不但順利經
營，更和街坊建立了深厚的
情感。真好啊！

The store ran smoothly during this period
and we established meaningful relationship
with our neighbours. It feels great!

但没想到，熱鬧的街道不知不覺就變化起來。

Unexpectedly, sudden changes are found on this bustling street.

常客好像減少了；店舖開始被
淘汰；連街坊的身影也少見。

Regular customers have decreased;
shops began to close, and even some
of the neighbours have left.

但我依然相信，這裏就
是維繫人和情的地方。

I still believe that this is the
place where human touch is
valued.

所以，即使附近的老店逐漸消失……

Therefore, even though old shops nearby are disappearing...

舊大廈被清拆，街坊搬走……

Buildings are being demolished, neighbours are moving out...

我也會堅持守護媽媽的雜貨店，
好好保留潮州文化。
I will stay and mind my Mum's grocery store
to preserve Teochew culture.

九龍城的潮州生活圈
Little Teochew in Hong Kong

九龍城是潮州人的集中地，更有「小潮州」之稱，特別是衙前塱道，每隔幾步便有一間潮州店。這個景象背後原因可以追溯到二次大戰後，當時，不少潮州人逃離來香港，聚居於九龍城一帶，並在這裏開設潮州雜貨店、潮州菜館等，當中有些至今已屹立逾半世紀，由家族成員或員工接任傳承，以延續這區之獨特潮州文化及人情味。

隨着寨城清拆、啟德機場搬遷，九龍城的潮州人口越來越少，我們期望可以透過此繪本，讓小朋友深入淺出了解一些潮州的飲食文化與習俗，同時令這種文化得以承傳。

Kowloon City is a hub for Teochew people, also known as 'Little Teochew', especially along Nga Tsin Long Road where Teochew shops are found every few steps. This phenomenon can be traced back to the post–World War II era when many Teochew people fled to Hong Kong and settled in Kowloon City. They opened Teochew grocery stores and restaurants in this area. Some of them have stood for over half a century, passed down through family members or employees, preserving a unique Teochew culture and warmth in this region.

With the demolition of the Kowloon Walled City and the relocation of the Kai Tak Airport, the population of Teochew people in Kowloon City has decreased significantly. Through this picture book, we hope to provide children with an idea of Teochew culinary culture in an easily understandable manner, promoting the inheritance of this unique cultural heritage.

躍變 · 龍城——
九龍城主題步行徑

由市區更新基金資助，躍變 · 龍城——九龍城主題步行徑於2018年1月1日起正式營運，為期7年，步行徑全長約6.5公里，分為5個特色路段，北端以九龍寨城公園為起點，途經宋皇臺、土瓜灣，連接南端的紅磡聖母堂。項目團隊透過改善及美化路段上的硬件設施、舉辦活動、設立訪客中心等連結區內的居民及持份者，以延續及推廣九龍城區的文化歷史。

步行徑社區繪本

步行徑出版一系列繪本，分為九龍城、土瓜灣、紅磡三個篇章，讓區內的幼稚園學生及家長認識社區。我們希望讀者透過繪本，了解步行徑不同路段的歷史文化，並認識步行徑上不同公共設施的硬件知識。

香港聖公會福利協會

聖公會於1843年開基。其後，聖公會已在九龍城區興建聖堂與學校，提供社會服務，照顧老弱孤幼，至今180多年，見證社區變化。1966年，香港聖公會福利協會成立，專責提供社會服務。「躍變 · 龍城——九龍城主題步行徑」為福利協會近年的重點項目，延續聖公會對九龍城的承擔與情懷。

Kowloon City in Transformation – Kowloon City Themed Walking Trail

Supported by the Urban Renewal Fund, the 7-year Kowloon City Themed Walking Trail project began operation on 1st January, 2018. The 6.5 km Walking Trail is divided into 5 routes with different characteristics, stretching from Kowloon Walled City Park to its north, and St Mary's Church in Hung Hom to its south. The Walking Trail team has renewed and upgraded various hardware facilities, organised activities and set up an information centre to connect with residents and stakeholders, prolong and promote the history of Kowloon City.

Picture Books on the Walking Trail

The Walking Trail publishes a series of picture books on Kowloon City, To Kwa Wan and Hung Hom for students and parents of kindergartens in the districts. With these books, we hope to help readers understand the history and culture of different sections of the walking trail, and learn about its public facilities and hardware.

Hong Kong Sheng Kung Hui Welfare Council

Sheng Kung Hui started its presence in Hong Kong in 1843, soon, Sheng Kung Hui established churches and schools in Kowloon City, providing social services and taking care of the elderly, people in need and orphans. It had been witnessing changes in the community for 180 years. In 1966, Hong Kong Sheng Kung Hui Welfare Council was established to provide social services particularly. Kowloon City in Transformation – Kowloon City Themed Walking Trail is a key project of the Welfare Council in recent years, continuing Sheng Kung Hui's love and care for Kowloon City.